Russell's
Christmas
Magic

Rob Scotton

HarperCollins *Children's Books*

Special thanks to Maria

First published in hardback by HarperCollins Publishers, USA, in 2007
First published in paperback in Great Britain by HarperCollins Children's Books in 2007
This edition published in 2009

1 3 5 7 9 10 8 6 4 2

ISBN-13: 978-0-00-731726-4

HarperCollins Children's Books is a division of HarperCollins Publishers Ltd.

Text and illustrations copyright © Rob Scotton 2007

Typography by Martha Rago

Visit our website at: www.harpercollins.co.uk

Printed and bound in China

www.robscotton.com

For my family and yours
—R.S.

'TWAS the night before Christmas in Frogsbottom Field. Not a creature was stirring,

except for…

Russell. As he was hanging the very last lantern on the old tree, a shooting star caught his eye.

Closer and closer it came.

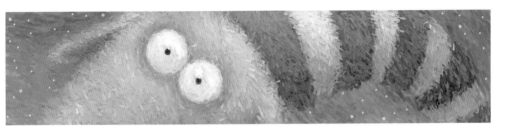

Brighter and brighter

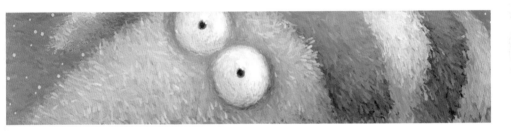

and then…

WHOOOSH!

The shooting star snuffed out the lanterns and came down somewhere in Firefly Wood.

"Now Christmas is ruined," Russell groaned…

and he trudged off to investigate.

He came upon a small, round man brushing snow from his belly.

"Santa!" Russell exclaimed.

"You see! You see!
You shouldn't see me," Santa said.
"The sleigh is broken and so
is the Christmas Spell.

Christmas
must be
cancelled!"

The sleigh was beyond repair.

"First Christmas is ruined and now it's cancelled," said Russell.

WHAT'S
A SANTA
TO DO?

An idea bounced around in Russell's hat and settled on his head.

He raced to his workshop, grabbed his tool chest and headed for a snowy mound.

Russell dug

and dug

until…

a rusty old car emerged.

"How can that help?" Santa asked and sighed.

So Russell welded this part to that.

He hammered and sawed

and banged and clattered.

SANTA

Finally he turned to Santa.

"Well?" Russell asked sheepishly.

"Russell, it... it's...
It's wondrous, magnificent – a thing
of beauty, a work of genius!" Santa gushed.

"Will it work?"

As Santa harnessed the reindeer to the new sleigh,
    they began
        to disappear.

"I can't see you!" said Russell.

"You see! You see!
You can't see me.
The sleigh is fixed and so
is the Christmas Spell," cried Santa.

"Christmas
is uncancelled!"

"Will you come with us?" asked Santa.

"Will we be gone for long?" asked Russell.

"For the blink of an eye!" he replied.

Russell felt for the sleigh and climbed aboard.

"I can see you again," he said to Santa.

"Of course! Now you're part of the Christmas Spell," cried Santa.

"Now, Dasher! Now, Dancer! Now, Prancer and Vixen!
On, Comet! On, Cupid! On, Donner and Blitzen!"

Up, up, higher and higher they flew.

Across land, across oceans they sped.

Through the magical Northern Lights they passed.

They visited all the children of the world
and left presents for each and every one.

In the blink of an eye they were back in Frogsbottom Field.
Santa waved his hand and presents appeared.

Santa gave Russell the very last present.

Inside was a tiny glass bauble.

Russell hung the ornament on the tree,
where it flickered and glowed.

Soon it shone with all the brilliance of the Northern Lights.

"It's a little bit of the Christmas Spell, just for you," said Santa.
"And now it's time, it's time to go."

"Goodbye, Russell, the sheep that saved Christmas," cried Santa.

"And Merry Christmas to you!"